# MONSTER KNOCK KNOCKS

By
**WILLIAM COLE & MIKE THALER**

**Cartoons by
MIKE THALER**

A MINSTREL® BOOK

PUBLISHED BY POCKET BOOKS

New York   London   Toronto   Sydney   Tokyo   Singapore

*DEADICATION*

**For Gwynn and all
my Albuquerque friends
who love knock knocks
M.T.**

 A Minstrel Book published by
POCKET BOOKS, a division of Simon & Schuster Inc.
1230 Avenue of the Americas, New York, NY 10020

Text copyright © 1982 by William Cole and Mike Thaler
Illustrations copyright © 1982 by Mike Thaler
Cover illustration copyright © 1982 by Mike Thaler

ISBN: 0-671-70653-5

First Minstrel Books printing January 1988

10  9  8  7  6  5  4  3

A MINSTREL BOOK and colophon are registered trademarks
of Simon & Schuster Inc.

Printed in the U.S.A.

**Knock knock.
Who's there?
Horror.**

**Horror who?**

# **Horror** ya doin'?

**Knock knock.**
**Who's there?**
**Terrorize.**

**Terrorize who?**

## She couldn't **terrorize** away from me!

**Knock knock.**
**Who's there?**
**Giant squid.**

**Giant squid who?**

**Giant squid** when they're ahead.

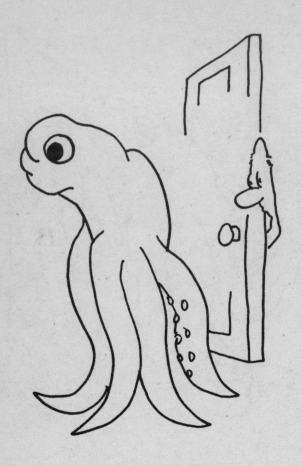

**Knock knock!**
**Who's there?**
**Frankenstein.**

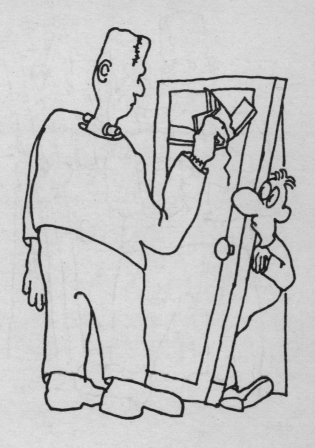

**Frankenstein who?**

**Frankenstein** *of root beer makes a good lunch.*

**Knock knock.**
**Who's there?**
**Zombies.**

**Zombies who?**

**Zombies** *make honey* *and* **zombies** *don't!*

**Knock knock.**
**Who's there?**
**Hound.**

**Hound who?**

**Hound** *the world did I change so much?*

**Knock knock.**
**Who's there?**
**Howl.**

**Howl who?**

**Howl** *I get in if you don't open the door?*

**Knock knock!!**
**Who's there?**
**Karloff.**

**Karloff who?**

# **Karloff** *your hounds!*

**Knock knock.
Who's there?
Eerie.**

**Eerie who?**

**Knock knock.
Who's there?
Coffin.**

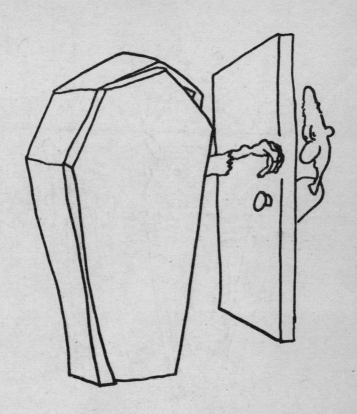

**Coffin who?**

# When you're **coffin,** cover your mouth!

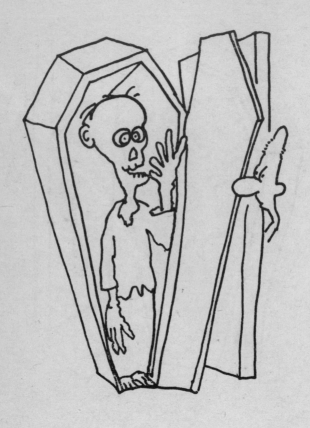

**Knock knock.**
**Who's there?**
**Groan.**

**Groan who?**

**Groan** *used to my face is difficult.*

**Knock knock.**
**Who's there?**
**Weirdo.**

**Weirdo who?**

**Weirdo** *you get all these bad jokes?*

**Knock knock.**
**Who's there?**
**Vampire.**

**Vampire who?**

**Vampire** *State's a tall building.*

**Knock knock.**
**Who's there?**
**Dracula.**

**Dracula who?**

## These are spec**Dracula** jokes!

**Knock knock.**
**Who's there?**
**Spider.**

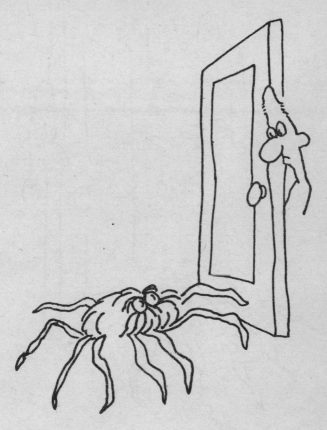

**Spider who?**

*I **spider** gettin' kissed behind the fence.*

**Knock knock.**
**Who's there?**
**Ogre and ogre.**

**Ogre and ogre who?**

# Kiss me **ogre and ogre** again!

**Knock knock.**
**Who's there?**
**Vader.**

**Vader who?**

*The **Vader** will come with the menu soón.*

**Knock knock.**
**Who's there?**
**Evil.**

**Evil who?**

*Evil* come if you whistle.

**Knock knock.
Who's there?
Mummified.**

**Mummif**

*My **mummified** you a hamburger.*

**Knock knock.**
**Who's there?**
**Goblin.**

**Goblin** *your food is bad manners.*

**Knock knock.**
**Who's there?**
**Fangs.**

**Fangs who?**

**Fangs** *a lot for answering the door.*

Knock knock.
Who's there?
Gruesome.

Gruesome who?

*I **gruesome** since I saw you last.*

**Knock knock.**
**Who's there?**
**Macabre.**

**Macabre who?**

**Macabre** *still has corn on it.*

**Knock knock.
Who's there?
Hades.**

**Hades who?**

**Hades** are bad jokes.

**Knock knock.**
**Who's there?**
**Zombie.**

**Zombie who?**

**Zombie** *good jokes,* **zombie** *bad.*

**Knock knock.
Who's there?
Vaults.**

**Vaults who?**

Could I have the next **vaults,** please?

**Knock knock.**
**Who's there?**
**Thing.**

**Thing who?**

**Thing** *it over.*

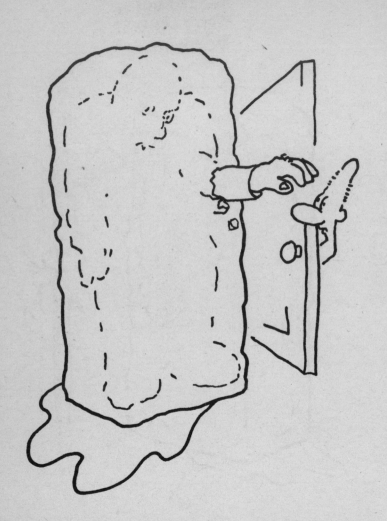

**Knock Knock.**
**Who's there?**
**Voodoo.**

**Voodoo who?**

**Voodoo** *you think you are?*

**Knock knock.**
**Who's there?**
**Beast.**

**Beast who?**

**Beast** *still; I'm tryin' to think.*

**Knock knock.**
**Who's there?**
**Jekyll and Hyde.**

**Jekyll and Hyde who?**

If your **Jekyll** bounce,
you'd better **Hyde**.

**Knock knock.**
**Who's there?**
**Jaws.**

**Jaws who?**

**Jaws** *wanted to say hello!*

**Knock knock.**
**Who's there?**
**Gorilla.**

**Gorilla who?**

**_Gorilla_** _me a cheese sandwich._

**Knock knock.**
**Who's there?**
**King Kong.**

**King Kong who?**

## A **King Kong** do no wrong.

Knock knock!!!
Who's there?
Godzilla.

Godzilla who?

*I* **Godzilla** *buckles on my shoes.*

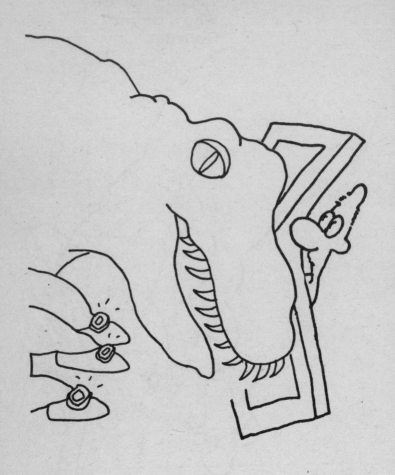

**Knock knock.**
**Who's there?**
**Torture.**

**Torture who?**

*I **torture** dog to shake hands!*

**Knock knock.**
**Who's there?**
**Gargoyle.**

**Gargoyle who?**

*If you **gargoyle** with salt water,
your throat will feel better.*

**Knock knock.**
**Who's there?**
**Minotaur.**

**Minotaur who?**

In a two **Minotaur** you can see the haunted castle.

**Knock knock.**
**Who's there?**
**Dinosaur.**

**Dinosaur who?**

**Dinosaur** *the haunted castle;*
*do you want to?*

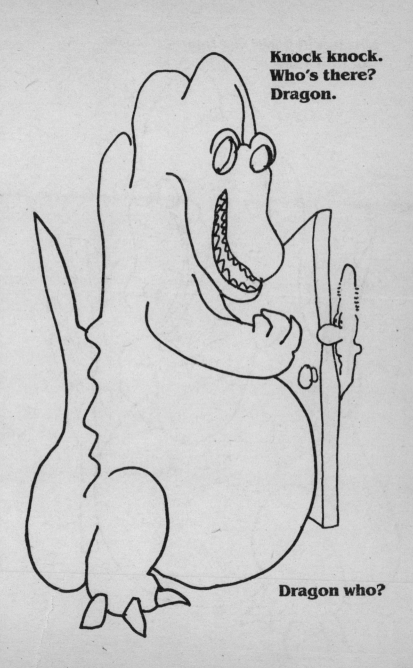

**Knock knock.**
**Who's there?**
**Dragon.**

**Dragon who?**

**Dragon** *in jokes like this
can ruin a book!*

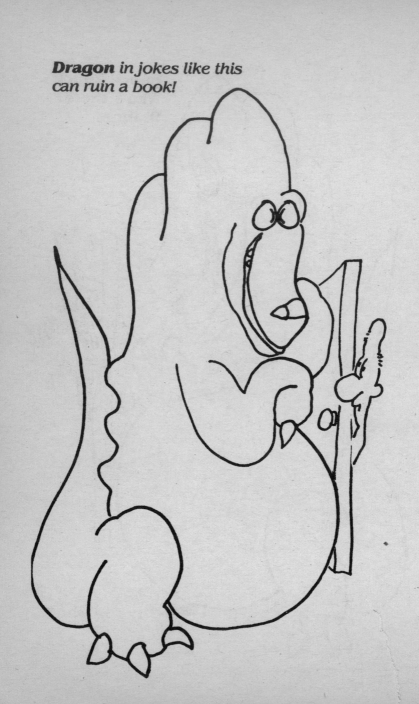

**Knock knock.
Who's there?
Lugosi.**

**Lugosi who?**

**Lugosi** *what's playin' at the movies.*

**Knock knock.
Who's there?
Monster.**

**Monster who?**

C'**monster** the stew; it's stickin' to the pot!

**Knock knock.
Who's there?
Caldron.**

**Caldron who?**

**Caldron** *heck standin' out here!*

**Knock knock.**
**Who's there?**
**Witches.**

**Witches who?**

**Witches** *the best knock knock of these?*

**Knock knock.**
**Who's there?**
**Viper.**

**Viper who?**

**Viper** *chin; she's droolin'.*

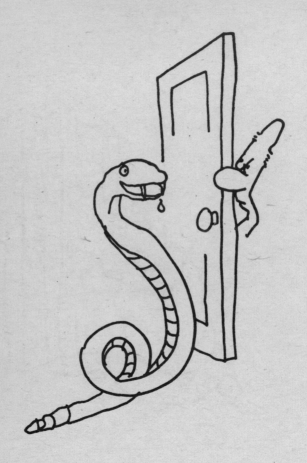

**Knock knock.**
**Who's there?**
**Martians.**

**Martians who?**

# Don't write on the **Martians!**

**Knock knock.**
**Who's there?**
**Constrictor.**

**Constrictor who?**

## Constrictor *teachers make us learn?*

**Knock knock.**
**Who's there?**
**Ghost.**

**Ghost who?**

***Ghost*** *stand in the corner.*

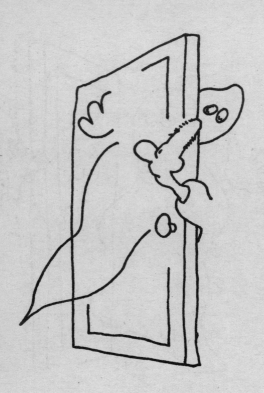

**Knock knock.**
**Who's there?**
**Cyclops.**

**Cyclops who?**

**Cyclops** along like a good horse.

**Knock knock.**
**Who's there?**
**Yeti.**

**Yeti who?**

*It's freezin', **yeti** keeps walking through the snow.*

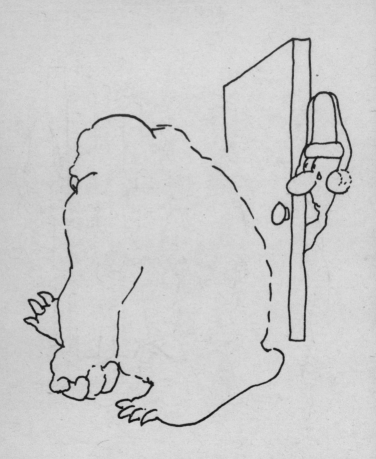

**Knock knock.**
**Who's there?**
**Creature.**

**Creature who?**

# *Creature* own knock knocks!

# About the Authors

WILLIAM COLE is an anthologist, a poet, and a writer; he's written and published over sixty books for both children and adults. He makes his home in New York City, where he has his own private library containing more than 5,000 books of poetry.

MIKE THALER is known as America's Riddle King. He is the creator of Letterman, the popular "Electric Company" character, and has earned a fine reputation as author and illustrator of over eighty children's books ranging from original riddle and joke books to fables and picture books. In addition, Mike has designed games and software discs, made recordings for Scholastic and Caedmon Records, and appeared in videos. *The Saturday Review* has called him "one of the most creative people in children's books today." His titles *Oinkers Away* and *Paws* will be available soon as Minstel Books.

In addition to his work with children's books, Mike spends much of his time sculpting, drawing, and songwriting. He is a sought-after speaker and has given many programs and workshops for children and adults across the country.

Above all, he believes in creativity—in himself and in others. "That is," says Mike, "my life and my work."